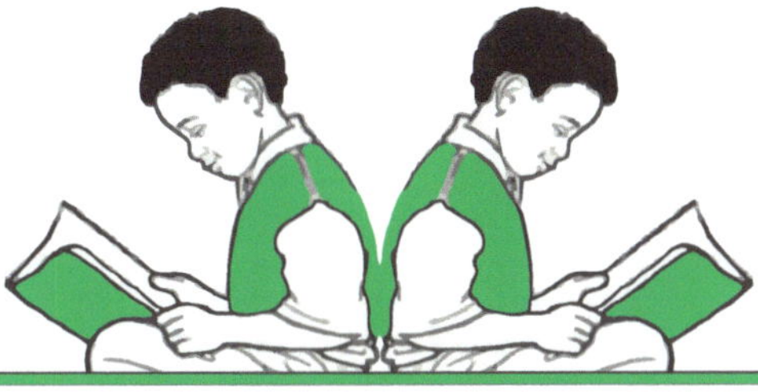

THIS BOOK BELONGS TO

Icon Publishing Limited
P. O. Box OD 972
Odorkor, Accra
Ghana
www.facebook.com/myicongh
www.twitter.com/myicongh
+233 (0)23 3505 055,

iconpublishingltd@gmail.com
iconpublishing@ymail.com
enquiries.icongh@gmail.com

Books published by Icon Publishing Limited are available at special discounts
for bulk purchases in Ghana by corporations, institutions, and other
organisations. For more information, please call the Special Markets
Department on +233 (0)23 3505 055 or send an e-mail to
iconpublishingltd@gmail.com.

Cover and Interior Design by iCON-gh +233 24 4890 432

ISBN: 978-9988-8567-1-7

ANANSE FINALLY MEETS HIS MATCH

AND ANOTHER TALE FROM AFRICA*

*Ananse and the Squirrel in Court

Dan Odei

Kwame Insaidoo

This Ghanaian folktale shows how the quality of our friends can either help us or betray us.

Many years ago Kwaku Ananse and his family lived in a town that had nothing to eat. The entire family was starving, and the wife pressured her husband Ananse to do whatever he had to do to provide food for the family.

Ananse had no choice but to leave home and travel to a distant land where he met an old friend who had plenty of food to eat.

The friend had a she-goat that produced whatever food he wanted, but he had to say the magic word that only the goat understood: *dabrekotwasuhoro*. With that, the goat responded by producing any kind of food one wanted to eat. Ananse and his friend had sufficient food to eat because the goat kept producing food for them. Ananse was grateful to his friend, but when he got ready to return home, he contrived a secret plan to steal the mild-mannered goat to feed his family. Ananse's friend became suspicious of his motives, however, so he also developed a counter plan.

The night before Ananse's departure, his friend went and got his neighbour, the tiger, to pretend to be the goat and sleep where the goat normally slept. Ananse never thought that his friend would play such a clever trick on him, so in the middle of the night, when all the people in the house were fast asleep, he eased himself to where the goat slept and slowly placed what he thought was the goat in a sack and carried it out of the house, without saying good-bye to his friend.

Ananse began humming melodious songs as he walked deep into the forest with the sack containing what he thought was the goat on top of his head. He felt quite pleased, as he believed that his family would soon be fed with plenty of food.

As Ananse was about to get home, he addressed the animal in the sack by saying the magic word, *dabrekotwasuhoro,* but the "goat" scratched Ananse's head with one of his sharp claws and Ananse began to bleed. But the happy Ananse was unworried and simply told the tiger that he thought was the goat to be quiet and patient because they were almost safely home.

The tiger scratched Ananse's head with one of his sharp claws

When Ananse got home, he climbed his ladder, put the sack with the tiger inside on the roof of his house, and retired to his bed to get some much-needed rest. The next day Ananse sent his first son, Ntikuma, to go to the roof of the house and say *"dabrekotwa-suhoro"* to the goat, so she would produce all kinds of food for them to eat.

Ntikuma took a big pot with him and climbed up the roof, hoping to get abundant food for his family, but when he came face-to-face with the red, bloodshot eyes of the fierce tiger, he fell violently to the ground and broke his little legs while screaming, "Tiger! Tiger! Tiger!" But his father, who did not know that he had mistakenly brought the tiger to his rooftop, scolded Ntikuma. "You are a useless boy because when you see a productive she-goat, you call it a tiger. Get out of my way and let your hardworking junior brother go up there and bring us some delicious food."

In a fit of anger, Ananse sent his junior son, a bold and no-nonsense person who was feared by all the village kids, whom he bullied. The junior son courageously climbed the ladder to the rooftop, hoping to get all kinds of food from the goat, but he was so frightened by the wild-looking tiger ready to pounce on him that he fell from the rooftop and hurt his head so badly that he began to scream for help.

Ananse was so disgusted with the cowardly attitudes of his children that he asked his wife, "What kinds of children do you have? Look at their cowardly attitudes when all they had to do was go to the roof and bring us some delicious food from a mere harmless goat who is just a bit different from other normal goats. Why don't you go and find out what these children are foolishly running away from?"

Without saying a word his wife boldly climbed up to the roof to find out what her husband was talking about and why her children were so frightened and were falling down from the rooftop. Before the wife reached the roof, she saw a wild tiger with red eyes and sharp claws, looking down menacingly at her like he had seen his prey.

Ananse's wife fell down shouting and screaming to her husband, "You better go there and see that your so-called she goat is really a tiger. You have been duped. You better go up there and calm him down, or he'll eat all of us today."

Ananse thought his family had gone crazy to tell him that the goat he had brought home was actually tiger, so he climbed up the ladder and went to the roof to find out what was actually up there. Sure enough, when Ananse got up there, he found himself face-to-face with a wild tiger who stared hard at him, but Ananse summoned all the courage at his disposal and apologetically said in a pleasant tone, "Oh, my friend, you know, I came here to see you because I have a message for you. Please come with me downstairs."

The tiger followed him downstairs to his house and sat besides Ananse and his family in the seat that Ananse directed him to. Then Ananse told the tiger he wanted his children to bring him the present he had concealed in the bush for the tiger. Ananse told Ntikuma to go into the bush and bring him his pipe, but before he left Ananse made a sign and said, "Look at his cowardly head, looking like a boy who will not come back home again with my pipe."

The son went into the bush and hid in the prearranged location his father had shown him and never came back. When Ananse waited for about five minutes and his elder son did not return, he

*Ananse found himself face-to-face with a wild tiger who stared
hard at him*

pretended he was angry because the boy had not returned, so he sent the junior son to go and find out what had happened to his brother and to bring back the big, expensive gift for their guest, the tiger.

As the junior son left, Ananse added, "Look at his rickety legs and how he walks like he will not come back to this dangerous house again."

The junior son got the message and didn't return once he got into the bush. The tiger sat by Ananse and wife with his fierce eyes blazing, while licking his lips, knowing that he was going to eat Ananse and his family. He did believe, however, that Ananse's sons would return to save their parents, so he waited, knowing that they would certainly return with his big expensive gift and then he would eat them for his dinner.

Ananse told his wife to go and see what the children were doing in the bush that was taking them so long, but before she left, Ananse spoke to her in such a way that she understood that she was not to come back. He said, "Look at my beautiful wife, walking and shaking her hips like she will not come back to me again." She understood the sarcasm in her husband's voice, so she joined her children in their hideout and didn't return.

Ananse and the tiger sat there in absolute silence, waiting for Ananse's family to return to the house, but they waited in vain. Ananse told the tiger to have some patience because he believed that something bad might have happened to his family. They were a respectful and obedient family, and he could not understand why they had not returned to the house yet. Ananse begged the tiger to give him just one minute to go find out what was keeping his family in the bush. He promised that he would return with his family and the tiger's gift. Ananse left and went to the prearranged destination where his family was patiently waiting for him.

When Ananse saw his family he told them, "We were lucky to get away from that monster. The tiger is determined to have us for his dinner tonight, and we must hurry to an old cave near the foothills of the mountain to the west of our village." They left and stayed in the cave for two days and did not come out, but the tiger was determined to let Ananse know that he could not fool him this time and that he would find and eat him at all costs.

The tiger began screaming and shouting for Ananse to come back, "Ananse, you better come out because, sooner or later, I am going to get you. You might as well come out now and save all of us the anguish and trouble of violently catching you!" But Ananse and his family were so fearful that they dared not respond.

The tiger devised an old trick that he used against his enemies. He put four stones in a fire until they were red hot, and then he took the first stone and said, "This hot red stone is for the head of Ananse's first son." And with that he threw the stone in the direction of the cave, and the stone hit Ananse's first son's head. When the son began to cry, Ananse and his wife quieted him down, saying, "Do you want this monster to get us?"

The tiger threw the second stone for Ananse's second son, and it hit his head as well, but Ananse calmed him down too. And when the stone hit his wife, Ananse covered her mouth with his hand so tightly that the wife could not cry. The last red hot stone hit Ananse on his right cheekbone, and Ananse burst out crying and told all his family members to cry too. When the tiger heard them crying he called to

Ananse, "You must surrender now because I know where you are, and I am going to eat you up now, so you better come out."

Ananse and his family were surprised that the tiger was still on the prowl, looking to get them, so they ran through the bush to get away from the tiger. Eventually, they came to a small hut where an old lady was making her pottery. Ananse begged the old lady, "Please … We need your help. The tiger wants to eat us, and we desperately need a hideout." The old lady had mercy on Ananse and his family and asked them to get into a dirty pot lying in the gutter behind her hut.

Scarcely had they hidden in the pot, than the tiger arrived, panting, with his red eyes looking for Ananse. He asked the old lady to tell the truth about whether she had seen Ananse and his family, but the loyal lady responded that she had not seen them. The smart tiger, sensing that the old lady was lying to him, offered to buy a pot from her, and he insisted that the dirty pot lying in the gutter behind the hut was the one pot he just had to buy. When the old lady protested, the tiger growled, showed his sharp teeth, and opened his red blood-shot eyes very wide. He

The tiger arrived, panting, with his red eyes looking for Ananse

demanded she allow him to buy the dirty pot. The old lady, fearing for her life, quickly sold the dirty pot to the tiger.

The tiger picked up the dirty pot and moved it slowly to a small cave, knowing that when he opened it, Ananse and his family would come out and he would have his dinner for the day. Ananse knew that the tiger would kill him and his family, so he thought hard and began chewing a lot of hot red peppers in his mouth waiting for the tiger to open the pot.

The tiger eventually opened the pot and peered into it with his eyes opened wide. When Ananse saw the tiger's wide-open eyes, he spat the hot pepper he had been chewing into the tiger's eyes, momentarily blinding the tiger. Ananse and his family took their opportunity and ran away from the tiger. The tiger never saw them again.

Moral Lessons

The main moral here concerns the quality of friends we have. If Ananse had been a true friend, he would have acted like one, but instead we saw how poorly he treated his so-called friend because he was not a true friend. Ananse's friend was a good person and a good friend to Ananse; when Ananse was hungry, he called him to his house, fed him for many days, showed him kindness, and made sure that Ananse did not starve in his time of need. We should all strive to be of character, like Ananse's friend, giving help to our friends, not because we want anything in return, but because it is the right thing to do.

Ananse proved that he was not a good friend, but selfish and concerned for himself only. Had he been a good friend, he would have asked his friend to give him some food to carry home to his family rather than stealing his friend's lone, valuable goat. Ananse was not a good friend because he had no problem depriving his friend of his means of livelihood by stealing from him. For the kindness his friend showed him, Ananse showed that he was a mean-spirited person, not worthy of friendship. We should learn to shy away from "friends" like Ananse.

Answer the following questions:

1. What magic word did the she-goat only understand?

2. a) What plan did Ananse contrive?

   b) What counter-plan did Ananse's old friend develop?

3. a) What happened when Ntikuma climbed up the roof of the house to get some food for the family?

   b) What happened to Ananse's wife and his junior son in quick successions when they climbed up the roof?

4. Describe how Ananse managed to get the whole family including himself out of the room where the tiger was waiting?

5. What old trick did the tiger devise to hunt Ananse's family?

6. Describe how Ananse saved his family from the dirty pot?

7.   What have you learned from this folktale?

8.   Find the meaning of the following words in the dictionary and use them in sentences of your own,

i. Contrived

ii. Humming

iii. Retired

iv. Fierce

v. Violently

vi. Courageously

vii. Disgusted

viii. Menacingly

ix. Prey

x. Duped

xi. Stared

xii. Apologetically

xiv. Anguish

xv. Dared

xvi. Devised

xvii. Prowl

xviii. Desperately

xix. Protested

xx. Growled

xxi. Momentarily

Ananse and the Squirrel in Court

In this Ghanaian folktale the trickster Ananse deceives the squirrel, his best friend, and steals his farm.

Once upon a time, there was a big famine in the land. Nobody had any food to eat, and the only thing available to drink was water, water, and only water. Ananse and the squirrel were best friends who did almost everything together; they shared the little food and water they received with each other, and slept in the same house.

One lucky day a rich farmer came to their village and, feeling sorry for Ananse and the squirrel because of the deplorable and miserable conditions they were living under, offered each of them a big bucket full of corn.

Ananse roasted his entire bucket of corn and ate it all over a period of two weeks, but the squirrel decided to divide his corn into two parts. He roasted one half of the corn and planted the other half in a large farm in the middle of the thick forest, where no one would be able to locate it. The squirrel made no road or path to his farm but just climbed trees and walked across branches to reach his farm so no one would know about it. The squirrel did not tell Ananse about the existence of his farm because he knew that Ananse was ruthlessly cunning and would do anything to seize it.

Meanwhile, Ananse had finished eating all his corn and began starving again, so he resorted to drinking water from morning until night and going to bed with only water in his belly. The thoughtful squirrel's corn was beginning to grow, and the squirrel was slowly enjoying the fruits of his hard labour. Soon he would banish hunger and poverty forever from his life, because he vowed that he would always save some seeds to plant during the lean periods. The squirrel was looking good and well fed despite the hunger in the land.

Ananse was surprised to see the squirrel looking so good despite the devastating famine in their land, so he decided to tiptoe secretly behind the squirrel to find out where he was getting his nourishment. As the squirrel was going to his farm early one morning,

Ananse secretly followed him and to his amazement and delight saw a huge farm with a lot of ripened corn. When the squirrel left, Ananse spent two days making a wide path from his house to the farm and then began eating the corn more than twenty times a day. Every day, Ananse boldly walked with his family on the wide path he had made to the squirrel's farm, and they all openly ate the ripened corn until they were satisfied.

The squirrel was alarmed to see the rapid rate at which his corn farm was diminishing, so he decided to find out what was going on. He hid all day long in the middle of the farm to find out who was stealing his corn, and to his amazement he saw his own friend Ananse walk boldly on a wide well-paved path to his farm and then begin to eat his corn.

The squirrel jumped out of his hiding place, ready to kill Ananse with a big stick, but he thought otherwise. Instead he sternly told Ananse that he would see him in court. Ananse shouted, "Hey, Squirrel! You are the thief who stole my farm! This corn farm belongs to me, and you stole it! I will see you in court myself, you little devil!"

*The squirrel jumped out of his hiding place, ready to kill Ananse
with a big stick*

The next day the whole court room was packed with the squirrel's sympathizers, who wanted real justice for him. Most wondered how the cunning Ananse would be able to exonerate himself after being caught red-handed stealing the squirrel's corn.

The squirrel presented his case, telling the court how he had caught Ananse red-handed in his corn farm, eating some of the corn and bagging more of it to take to his house. The squirrel showed some of the stolen bags of corn to the judge.

The judge asked Ananse whether he was guilty of stealing the squirrel's corn, and transporting bags of corn away from his farm without his authorization. Ananse answered that he was not guilty. He said, "The squirrel is lying. The farm does not belong to him; it is mine. Squirrel is the intruder—not me!" Ananse swore that after he won the case he would countersue the squirrel for making false and malicious accusation against him.

Then Ananse shouted, "Your honour, I have spent a long time and a lot of money making my farm and have paved a wide path from my house to my farm, which I tend on a daily basis. I am upset and annoyed by the fact that a thief like the squirrel can claim my

Ananse talking to the judge

farm as his. Your honour, ask the squirrel, if the farm belongs to him, how he gets to his farm from his house. Let him prove to the court that he has paved a path or anything from his house to his own farm."

The judge asked the squirrel to answer Ananse's question on how he got to his farm. The squirrel answered that he climbed trees and walked across branches to go to his farm.

Ananse retorted before the crowded court, "Ridiculous! Your honour, how could he have the audacity to stand before your highness and tell you and the rest of us that he goes to his own hard-earned farm by climbing trees and bushes? What an absurd and shameful statement to tell this August court. Your honour, it is an insult to your authority for the squirrel to tell you such a cock-and-bull story here today and perjure himself before your mighty court."

The court found it impossible to accept that the squirrel could merely climb trees to get to the farm, so Ananse was awarded the farm along with all the corn growing on it. Ananse thanked the court and informed everyone present that he had decided, out of his own kindness, to forgive the squirrel for all his false statements and for attempting to impugn

Ananse's integrity and assassinate his character. He told the squirrel to be of good character and to "go out and sin no more."

Moral Lessons

The main moral of this story is that we should all be careful regarding our property and learn to get all the correct and legitimate paperwork that shows that we are the rightful owners of everything that we work so hard for. We should also be careful of friends like Ananse who are really cheats and do not have our best interests at heart and who only come to us for what they can get for themselves.

Answer the following questions:

1.   What was the only consumable available on the land?

2.   Why did the rich farmer feel sorry for Ananse and his squirrel friend?

3.   What did Ananse do with his entire bucket of corn?

4.   a) Where did the squirrel situate his farm and why did he keep it hidden from Ananse?

     b) How did the squirrel get to his farm on daily basis?

5.   a) How did Ananse find out about the squirrel's secret farm?

     b) How did he make his way to the farm?

6.   How did the squirrel find out someone was eating his ripened corn?

7.   How did Ananse steal the squirrel's farm?

8.   a) Why did the judges trust Ananse?

     b) What was the judges' final verdict?

9.   What have you learned from this folktale?

10. Lookup the meaning of the following words, and then use them in sentences of your own:

     I. Famine   ix. Exonerate

     ii. Deplorable   x. Intruder

iii. Miserable

iv. Ruthlessly

v. Cunning

vi. Devastating

vii. Diminishing

viii. Sternly

11. What are the meaning of the following idiomatic expressions?

i. to be caught red-handed;

ii. to assassinate one's character;

iii. a cock-and-bull story.

12. Give synonyms for the underlined words in the following sentences:

i. He was in the middle of the <u>thick</u> forest where no one would be able to <u>locate</u> it.

ii. Ananse was <u>surprised</u> to see the squirrel looking so good.

iii. To his <u>amazement</u> and <u>delight</u> Ananse saw a <u>huge</u> farm with a lot of ripened corn.

iv. Ananse <u>boldly</u> walked with his family into the farm.

v. The squirrel was <u>alarmed</u> to see the <u>rapid</u> rate at which his corn-farm was diminishing.

13. List ALL the adjectives that can be found in paragraphs two and three.